For:

_____

From:

_____

Library of Congress Control Number: 2022930814
ISBN 978-0-06-298571-2

22 23 24 25 26   RTLO   10 9 8 7 6 5 4 3 2 1

First Edition

Spring Sings
for The Grouchy Ladybug

HARPER

An Imprint of HarperCollins*Publishers*

Spring
is
here!

And all around,
there are many exciting new

sights

and

sounds.

Ducks
swimming
in the pond.

Frogs

hopping

on lily pads.

Turtles **peeking** their heads out of their shells.

Bunnies
nibbling
on yummy carrots.

Birds
calling out
their happy songs.

Bees
looking
for a
sweet treat.

Butterflies

dancing

through the air.

Baby chicks
hatching
from their eggs.

Spring

is here,

so shout

HOORAY!

Even

The Grouchy Ladybug

is smiling today!